Hucklebug

Written by Stephen Cosgrove
Illustrated by Robin James

A Serendipity™ *Book*

PSS!
PRICE STERN SLOAN

Dedicated to Kevin McCarthy,
the King of 'Splatz' and all
the other buggs that buzz about.

— Stephen

Far beyond the horizon, in the middle of the Coral Sea was the magical island of Serendipity. It was here that lived all the life-sized creatures from your dreams and imagination: unicorns, dragons, bunnies and bears.

Here, too, lived the small and tiny creatures like miniature winged horses, butterflies and smaller still, ant-like creatures called Hucklebugs. The Hucklebugs lived in a small village, just beyond the hedge at the farthest corner of someone's back yard. It was here, not long ago, that Berry Hucklebug was born. And it was here that Berry grew from a itty-bitty, baby bug to a tiny fun-loving almost grown-up bug.

Berry Hucklebug loved to play with the other young bugs of the village. They played Hucklebug hide 'n' seek, Hucklebug hopscotch, and Hucklebug tag.

Berry Hucklebug didn't really have a favorite game. He loved to play them all, and for years and years all he did was play.

One day Berry's father sat him down on a broad, green leaf and said, "Berry, you are old enough now to help with the chores of the village. There is food to be gathered for the winter and all Hucklebugs who are able must help."

"Me?" said an unbelieving Berry. "But I don't want to. I want to stay with my friends. I want to run and play in the sunshine."

Sternly, Berry's father looked down at him and said, "Everyone must work in this village and you are no exception. You will start tomorrow morning!"

Sadly, Berry walked back toward his Hucklebug friends, but his father's demands lay heavily on his mind and he really didn't feel like playing. So instead he went to his room and pouted. "What am I going to do?" he said. "I don't want to work, I want to play."

Suddenly an idea came to him. "I know," he said. "I'll run away and live by myself. Nobody will bother me then." With that, Berry rummaged through his butterfly wings and old bumblebee tails until he found his yellow bandana. Carefully he laid it on the floor and began packing.

He packed his hand-knitted antenna warmers for cold winter mornings. He packed his favorite red T-shirt with the big, bold, gold "B". And last, but not least, he packed his new orange sneakers for special occasions. Then Berry tied his bandana into a big, careful knot, threw it over his shoulder and slipped away from the village.

The farther he went from the village, the happier Berry became. There were beautiful flowers all around him. He saw forests of green grasses, and a blue sky overhead. "What do I need of that old village?" he laughed brightly. "Out here I have everything I need and," he giggled, "there's no one to tell me what to do."

He had traveled deep into the forest of grass when he happened upon one of his fellow Hucklebugs gathering food for the village. As soon as Berry saw him, he quickly hopped from the trail and hid from view. From his hiding place he watched as the worker bug carried a heavy bag of food back to the village.

"Better him than me," laughed Berry as he hurried on his way.

After a time, Berry came to a rise in the path. Creeping slowly to the top, he discovered a furry caterpillar slowly crawling along. Down below him he saw a gigantic house with a gigantic lawn and gigantic toys scattered about. "Wow!" exclaimed Berry. "I bet it would be a lot of fun to play there!"

The caterpillar twisted up and looked sternly at the runaway ant. "If you're thinking of going down there, little bug," he grumbled, "I'd think again."

Berry just laughed and twisted the caterpillar's antenna together like a pair of old knitted socks. Then he raced down the hill to the huge house below.

"That old, dumb caterpillar didn't know what he was talking about," he laughed. "Nobody will ever tell me what to do again!"

He ran, jumped and giggled onto the gigantic lawn, and there he found the most amazing toys that he'd ever seen in his entire life. There were monstrous squirt guns, and mammoth baseball gloves big enough for him to live in if he wished. He saw a beach ball that seemed a lebinty-million miles high. Berry felt as though he had found ant heaven.

Berry carefully climbed to the top of the beach ball and began bouncing up and down. He was doing flips and jumping so high he didn't notice as the back door of the gigantic house swung open.

Some giant kids were coming outside to play!

A gigantic tennis shoe kicked at the ball and it went flying!

Berry went flying!

Shaken, Berry picked himself up from the freshly-mowed grass. "What was that?" he asked. Slowly he turned and looked up and up and up, and for the first time saw the giants. "Wow! They're pretty big, but maybe they'll let me play."

With that he ran over to join in their fun.

"Hey, big kids!" he shouted from the ground below. "Can I play too?" The giants were so busy laughing and giggling that they didn't even hear him.

Just by chance, one of the giant boys spotted Berry standing in the grass. Carefully he leaned down and looked Berry right in the eye. "What a funny-looking bug," he said. "Hey, guys! Look at the weird-looking ant!"

Now let me tell you, Berry was more than a little bit scared. In fact, he was a lot scared.

Faster than you can say "Hucklebugs eat huckleberry pie," Berry was on his way. He ran up and over the giant's feet and on to the open grass beyond. Quicker than quick he was into the deeper grass.

From behind he could hear the heavy footsteps as the giants tried to follow. Berry was scared and that made him run faster as he scrambled over a leaf and under a twig, tearfully making his escape up the path.

Puffing and panting, Berry ran all the way back up to the top of the hill. There he found the old caterpillar still trying to untie his antennae. Once he was sure that the giants weren't following Berry helped the caterpillar fix his twisted antennae.

"You were right, Mr. Caterpillar," said Berry. "I shouldn't have gone down there. I've made a mess of things. I don't know what to do. I shouldn't have gone down to the giant's house and I shouldn't have run away from home. Now I am ashamed to go back." Berry felt so bad that he began to cry large, purple Hucklebug tears.

The wise old caterpillar smiled a little smile and said, "Little Hucklebug, if you have learned from your mistake, it is not a mistake, but a lesson. As you grow older you will make other mistakes, but never be afraid to admit them. Go back to the village now and do what needs to be done."

Berry wiped a tear from his eye, and then, thanking the caterpillar for his kindness, he headed home to the Hucklebug village.

Resolved to set things right he ran back down the path to the village. There, he bravely marched up to his father and said, " I'm really sorry I ran away. I've learned from my mistake, and it is a lesson I will always remember. I promise that I'll never run away again."

His father gave him a big hug and told him that he was forgiven. Since he had run away, though, he would have to work a little bit on Saturday as punishment.

Then his father smiled and said that since it was so late Berry could play for the rest of the day.

MISTAKES ARE ALWAYS MISTAKES,

OR SO I'VE HEARD THEM SAY.

BUT IF IT TEACHES A LESSON,

THE MISTAKE WILL GO AWAY.

Serendipity™ Books

Created by
Stephen Cosgrove and Robin James

Enjoy all the delightful books in the Serendipity™ Series:

Available wherever books are sold.

PSS!
PRICE STERN SLOAN